WHEN
JENNY LOST
HER SCARF

Written and Illustrated by
Esther Averill

Harper & Brothers, New York

O, happy
Are we
On our
Annual Spree.

—FROM AN OLD
MARCHING SONG
OF THE CAT CLUB

WHEN JENNY LOST HER SCARF

One fine spring day the little black cat, Jenny Linsky, sat at the open window of her house. Dreamily she watched her red scarf drying on a clothesline in the garden.

"I'm glad the housekeeper washed my scarf," thought Jenny. "Now it will be fresh and clean for me to wear to the Annual Spring Picnic of the Cat Club."

But all at once a rough dog, whom the club had christened "Rob the Robber," rushed out of a cellar, grabbed Jenny's scarf

and ran off with it. It happened so quickly that Jenny didn't have time to think or be scared. All she wanted was to get her scarf away from Rob. So she cut through the garden, climbed over the tall board fence and ran down the alley into South Street.

By sniffing the sidewalk, Jenny found the trail of the dog and the scarf. She followed the trail as far as the Toy and Catnip Shop

which stood
at the corner of the block.

Here Rob's trail turned sharply around the corner, into Mulligan Street.

"I guess he's taken my scarf to the Den of the Dogs," thought Jenny with a shiver.

She crept close to the Toy and Catnip Shop and peered cautiously down Mulligan Street toward the dark cellar where Rob and his band of dogs had their den. There was not a dog in sight.

"They're probably all inside, pawing my scarf," thought Jenny. "But I'll go into the den and get my scarf, even if they chew me up."

Fortunately, at this very moment, two friendly voices called out, behind her, "Jenny! Jenny Linsky! Wait for us!"

Jenny turned and saw the twin cats, Romulus and Remus, standing on the curb across the street. Of course she waited for them,

6

and when the traffic light turned from red
to green, the patchy-coated twins came
bounding over to her.

"Jenny, what has happened?" cried the
twins together. "What are you doing out in
the street, without your scarf?"

"That Rob the Robber stole it," replied
Jenny indignantly. And she told them what
had happened.

The twins said, "Well, Jenny, we admire
your spirit, but really you're no match for
Rob. Why don't you go home? We'll try to
get your scarf and bring it to the Cat Club
tonight."

The twins pushed Jenny with their speckled noses. She ran home and waited.

She waited all that afternoon; waited until the sun dropped in the west; waited until night descended and the cats began to gather beneath the maple tree that stood in the far corner of the Captain's garden. When they had formed a circle in front of their President, Jenny crept over to them.

Romulus and Remus had saved a place for

her between them, and as she squeezed into it they whispered to her, "No luck. No luck."

"Silence, please," ordered the President. "The meeting is about to open."

"But this is important, Mr. President," the twins objected. "It's about Jenny's scarf. It was stolen this morning."

Mr. President quickly opened the meeting.

"Jenny," he said gravely, "will you please step forward and tell us what happened?"

Shyly the little black cat stepped into the circle in front of Mr. President.

Jenny's neck felt cold and bare without

her red wool scarf tied snugly around it. And all those pairs of cat eyes staring at her through the moonlight frightened her. But she knew she had to speak. She must make the Cat Club understand how important was the scarf she had lost.

"Mr. President," said Jenny, "this morning Rob the Robber stole the red wool scarf my master, Captain Tinker, knit for me to wear wherever I go. Captain Tinker has gone off to sea on business. When he comes home, I don't want to have to tell him that I lost my scarf. I'll try my best to get it back."

"Thank you, Jenny. You may be seated," said Mr. President. "Romulus and Remus, kindly tell us what you know about this robbery."

As Jenny sat down, the twins stepped forward and explained how they had met Jenny and why they had sent her home.

"Then we followed Rob's trail to the Den of the Dogs on Mulligan Street," said the twins. "But Rob was guarding the door. He shouted to us that Jenny's scarf was hanging

on a nail in the den, and that a thousand cats could never get it back because the den would be guarded day and night."

"Thank you, Romulus and Remus," said Mr. President. "You may be seated, for I can see that Madame Butterfly wishes to speak."

As the twins returned to their seats, the club's most beautiful member, the silvery Madame Butterfly, stepped forward.

"This robbery bristles my whiskers," she declared. "At noon, while I was out shopping, I met Romulus and Remus. They told me all about it. Of course, I feel that what happened to Jenny this morning happened because of what happened here last Hallowe'en."

"Excuse me, Madame Butterfly," interrupted tough Sinbad. "What has what happened here last Hallowe'en got to do with our Annual Spring Picnic? Tonight the club's supposed to talk about our picnic plans."

"Patience, Sinbad," replied Butterfly. "I have a surprise for all of you. Look!"

Slowly Butterfly opened her silvery right front paw. Between two of its velvety pads lay a diamond, brighter than a star. Jenny's yellow eyes almost popped out of her head, and cries of *Oh!* and *Ah!* and *Please may I touch it?* went round the club.

Butterfly, guarding the diamond, said, "I have removed this jewel from the trimming on my nose flute, and I'm giving it to the club to pay for whatever it costs to get back Jenny's scarf. What's left over shall be spent on buying food for our picnic."

Sinbad asked, "Do you mean we can't have our picnic until we've found Jenny's scarf?"

"Exactly so," replied Butterfly. "Last Hallowe'en Jenny risked her life to bring me my flute, which I had lost. To do this, she had to outsmart Rob and all his dogs. Today Rob got even with Jenny by stealing her scarf. But I intend to help her get it back with this diamond."

Mr. President took the diamond happily, for there was not a penny in the treasury.

"Mr. President," cried Sinbad, "why not buy Jenny a new scarf, instead of waiting to get the old one back? Then we could hold our picnic on Saturday night, as we'd planned."

The members nodded. And Butterfly said,

"Jenny, shall you and I go to the Toy and Catnip Shop and try to buy a little scarf?"

"No," thought Jenny to herself. "All the diamonds in this city couldn't buy me anything as nice as my old red scarf. That was the first scarf I ever had."

But Sinbad was saying, "I know where we can buy fine fishes for a picnic—cheap."

"Oh!" sighed Jenny. "The club *does* want the picnic. Without the picnic, it won't seem to them like spring at all."

She raised her voice. "Thank you, Madame Butterfly. I'll go shopping with you."

So Butterfly took back the diamond and arranged to call for Jenny at ten o'clock next morning. And from breakfast until ten, Jenny polished her fur and whiskers for the shopping trip.

"Jenny, how nice you look!" said Butter-fly, when she arrived. "Come, let's start before those dogs get wind of our plans."

Side by side, the two cats crossed the garden, jumped over the fence, passed into South Street and dashed to the Toy and Cat-nip Shop. As they pushed open the door, the owner looked at them with surprise.

"My good woman," said Butterfly, "have you a red scarf for my young friend to wear?"

The woman did not seem to understand.

"Maybe a pink scarf," suggested Butterfly.

Again the owner failed to understand.

"Or a little blue scarf," said Butterfly, flashing the diamond she carried in her paw.

"Oh!" exclaimed the woman. "If you want to buy a toy for her, she might enjoy this duck." And she placed a big toy duck on the floor in front of Jenny.

"A duck to play with, when I need a scarf," thought Jenny miserably. But to be polite, she gave its tail a push.

"Quack!" shrieked the duck. "Quack! Quack!"

"Come, Jenny," said Butterfly in disgust. "If this store doesn't understand us, no store will. We might as well go home."

That night, at the club, Butterfly had to report that the shopping trip had failed. As she returned the diamond to Mr. President, she said, "There's nothing left to do but think of a way to get the old scarf back."

"Yes," agreed Mr. President, "let us close our eyes and think."

So they all closed their eyes and thought, but no one could think of a plan. When the meeting finally broke up, everyone felt blue. Saturday night was drawing near, and it looked as if there wouldn't be a picnic.

As Jenny paused in the window of her house, on her way to bed, she murmured, "The club has done everything it can to help. If we're to have the picnic, I must get help from somewhere else. But from whom?"

Suddenly she remembered her friend, the Fire Cat, Pickles, who worked in the Fire House on South Street. Pickles had once told her, "If you ever need me, let me know."

Jenny knew it wouldn't be much fun to travel on the streets at night, without her scarf to bring good luck. Perhaps those dogs would catch her. Never mind. She'd do the best she could. And without thinking of her own safety, she ran to the fence, jumped over it and sped down South Street toward the Fire House. Fortunately she reached it safely and found Pickles on duty.

"Jenny, what's the matter?" he asked.

"Rob the Robber stole my scarf," explained Jenny. "And he's hung it in the Den of the Dogs. The den is guarded so no cats can get in. And one thing has led to another. Now our club can't have its Annual Spring Picnic until we get back my scarf."

"I wish I could help you," said Pickles.

"Pickles," said Jenny, "you're a friend of the Fire Dog, Buster. He's a good dog, and maybe you could ask him to tell Rob to give me back my scarf."

"Buster's a very good dog," agreed Pickles. "But he works in a fire house way uptown. I won't see him until the Firemen's Ball in the summer. You run home, Jenny. It's long past your bedtime. I won't forget what you've told me. With dogs like those Mulligan ruffians, anything might happen."

It happened that same night, while Jenny was asleep in her basket in her upstairs bedroom, next to the street. She had been dreaming that the club was holding the picnic, and she was with them, eating a delicious fish, when she was awakened by the fire engines roaring along South Street.

Sleepily she thought of Pickles on the front seat of the hook and ladder—riding to

put out the fire. How safe she felt because of Pickles! How proud she was to know him! She was drifting back to sleep when she heard a *psst! psst!* beneath her window.

Jenny ran to the window and peered into the street.

On the sidewalk stood Romulus and Remus.

"The Den of the Dogs is on fire!" cried the twins. "Those dogs were playing with a box of matches they stole this afternoon. Jimminy whiskers! What a fire they started! We're going back to watch the blaze."

The twins dashed away and disappeared around the corner of the street.

"I must go, too," thought Jenny. "My red scarf is in the den. There's no time to lose. I'll take the short cut through the garden."

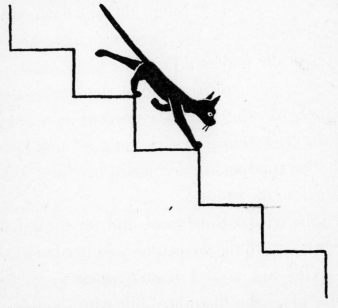

Jenny hurried down the stairs that led to the garden window. As her black paws sped from stair to stair, her mind kept saying, "My red scarf is in the den, and Pickles has gone over there to fight the fire. Pickles can save my scarf, but he'll be too busy to think of it himself. When I get there, I'll remind him."

Jenny leaped through the open window and ran across the garden to the fence. There she gathered her little black legs together and made ready to jump to the top of the fence. But when she tried to jump, her hind legs seemed to stick to the ground.

She tried again, and again her hind legs stuck to the ground.

She tried a third time, and for the third time something seemed to hold her back.

"It's just as if I wasn't meant to go to the fire," she thought. "But why shouldn't I go?"

Suddenly the reason became as clear to her as the moonlight on the grass. Pickles' duty was to fight the fire and keep it from spreading.

"I mustn't bother Pickles," Jenny decided. "I mustn't ask him to stop his noble work in

24

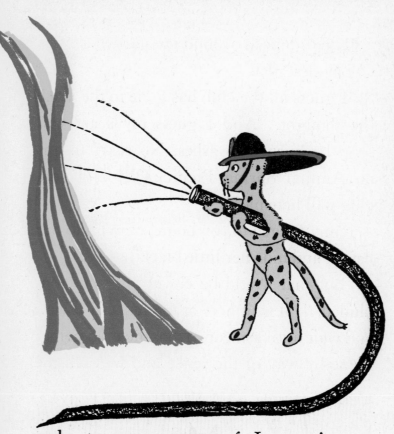

order to rescue my scarf. I mustn't even go and watch the fire, because if Pickles saw me he might remember my scarf and try to save it, when he shouldn't."

Jenny glanced around the garden. It was utterly deserted.

"I guess all the club has gone to the fire," she thought. "And I guess my scarf will soon be burned to ashes. No scarf means no Annual Spring Picnic. Oh! How the club will hate me!"

Jenny longed to run home, crawl into her basket and hide her little black face.

"But that would be cowardly," she concluded. "I'll wait here at the fence. I'll wait and wait until someone from the club comes home by way of the fence and will tell me

the news. Maybe Madame Butterfly will come, and I could beg her please not to think about a scarf for me, but to give all the diamond to the picnic."

At last Jenny could hear the hook and ladder returning slowly down South Street. The bell of the hook and ladder was ringing, "Fire's out! Fire's out!" And after a while she heard four paws turn into the alley.

"That's no one from the club," she thought. "I know the sound of all their paws."

Pit-pat! Pit-pat! The sound drew nearer and nearer. It was like the fire bell, saying *"Fire's out! Fire's out!"*

Jenny heard someone jump, and saw a huge spotted yellow paw clutch the top of the fence. Above the paw rose a shiny black helmet and a yellow face. Then came the left front paw, clutching something red.

"Catch!" boomed the Fire Cat.

Jenny reached up and caught the scarf. It hadn't been burned at all!

"Oh, thank you, Pickles! Thanks a thousand million times. Was anybody hurt?"

"Nobody hurt," replied Pickles. "But the den is flooded with water from the hose. I guess those dogs have learned a lesson."

"Pickles," said Jenny shyly, "with all you had to do, how did you remember my scarf?"

The Fire Cat laughed.

"At first I didn't have time to think of anything but helping the firemen squirt the hose," he said. "Then the Chief told me to rest. So I stopped and looked at the crowd. All the Cat Club was there—all but you."

"What did you think when you didn't see me?" asked Jenny.

"I thought of your scarf," answered Pickles.

"Oh, Pickles! I wish I could have helped you rescue it!" cried Jenny.

"You helped me best by staying home," said Pickles. "It takes courage for a little cat to wait patiently and unselfishly at home when her best red scarf is in a fire."

The Fire Cat raised his yellow paw, touched his helmet and saluted Jenny.

At that same moment, something moved toward her through the bushes. When she turned, Mr. President was standing on the moonlit grass, with all the members of the Cat Club.

"Jenny," began Mr. President, "our club is proud to see you honored by the Fire Department for your patience and unselfishness."

"Aye! Aye!" sang the members.

"We of the Cat Club also wish to honor you," said Mr. President. "We wish to honor you for this reason. Although you're small and shy, you always do the best you can."

Jenny's heart felt warm and happy.

"Jenny," continued Mr. President, "our club shall hold its Annual Spring Picnic on Saturday night in Washington Park, three blocks north of our garden. You, Jenny Linsky, wearing your red scarf, shall lead us as we march through the Arch of Victory that guards the entrance into the picnic grounds."